Walt Disney's

Cinderella

ADAPTED FROM THE FILM BY

Zoë Lewis

ILLUSTRATED BY

Robbin Cuddy

Disney
PRESS

NEW YORK

"Bibbidi-Bobbidi-Boo"
Words by Jerry Livingston.
Music by Mack David and Al Hoffman.
Copyright © 1948 Walt Disney Music Company. Copyright Renewed.
All Rights Reserved. Used by Permission.

Library of Congress Catalog Card Number: 94-70524
ISBN: 0-7868-3014-X / 0-7868-5008-6 (lib. bdg.)
FIRST EDITION
1   3   5   7   9   10   8   6   4   2

Walt Disney's Cinderella

Prologue

Once upon a time in a faraway land there was a tiny kingdom that was peaceful, prosperous, and rich in romance and tradition. There, in a stately château, lived a widowed gentleman with his little daughter, Cinderella. A kind and devoted father, he gave his beloved child every luxury and comfort. Still, he felt she needed a mother's care, and so he married again. For his second wife he chose a woman of good family with two daughters just Cinderella's age: by name, Anastasia and Drizella.

It was upon the untimely death of this good man, however, that the stepmother's true nature was revealed—cold, cruel, and bitterly jealous of Cinderella's charm and beauty. She was grimly determined to forward the interests of her own two awkward daughters.

As time went by, the château fell into disrepair. The family fortunes were squandered upon the vain and selfish stepsisters while Cinderella was forced to become a servant in her own home.

Yet through it all, Cinderella remained ever gentle and kind. With each and every dawn she found new hope that someday her dreams of happiness would come true. . . .

Chapter One

A beam of golden sunshine fell across Cinderella's bed as two bluebirds flew in through her open window.

"Cinderella," one bluebird chirped.

Cinderella sighed and rolled over, pulling a pillow over her head as she burrowed deeper under the covers.

"Cinderella," the other bird sang softly in her ear.

"Wake up!" chirped the first bird, poking its head under the pillow.

Cinderella reached out from under the covers and flicked the bluebird's tail. "Well, serves you right," she said to the startled bird. "Spoiling people's best dreams!" She laughed as the birds chirped and flew to the windowsill. "I know it's a lovely morning, but it was a lovely dream, too."

The birds whistled loudly.

Cinderella sat up and began to unbraid her shoulder-length blond hair. "What kind of a dream, you ask? It's a secret. Just like a wish, if you tell your dreams, they won't come true."

Cinderella sometimes thought her dreams were all that kept her from

sinking into despair. Ever since the death of her beloved father, Cinderella had been treated like a slave by her jealous stepmother— Lady Tremaine—and her nasty stepsisters, Anastasia and Drizella. They ordered her around, dressed her in rags, and forced her to do all their household chores. To forget her troubles, Cinderella often escaped into dreams of a happier life. She dreamed of falling in love . . . of being loved in return . . . of someday leaving her horrible home behind forever. And because her dreams were all she had, Cinderella never stopped believing in them.

Cinderella yawned and stretched. She smiled at the birds and mice

who had come into the room—they were the only real friends she had. Then she sighed as she heard the loud ringing of the palace clock tower. She got out of bed, went to the window, and glared at the majestic clock. "I hear you! 'Come on, get up,' you say! Even that clock orders me around," she said to the birds and mice. "Well, there's one thing no one can order me to do. They can't order me to stop dreaming."

The birds chirped in agreement.

"And perhaps someday," Cinderella said wistfully, "my wish will come true."

*   *   *

With the help of her animal friends, Cinderella quickly straightened her little room, which was located at the top of a steep, winding staircase in the château's highest tower. She made her bed and put on an old brown dress. Then she tied back her thick golden hair, put on her apron, and was ready to face another day of washing and scrubbing and listening to the demands of her stepfamily.

She was about to leave her bedroom when two mice darted under her door. Chattering excitedly, they scampered up to the top of the bureau, waving their arms frantically to attract Cinderella's attention.

"Wait a minute. One at a time, please," Cinderella told the mice patiently. She turned to one of them, a skinny mouse dressed in red. "Now, Jaq, what's all the fuss about?"

"There's a new mouse in the house," Jaq squeaked. "A visitor."

Cinderella smiled. "How nice," she said. She opened the drawer where she kept extra clothing for the mice. "He'll need a jacket . . . and shoes . . ."

The other mouse, who was dressed in blue, squeaked loudly.

"What's the matter, Luke?" Cinderella asked, concerned.

"We gotta get him out of the trap," Jaq blurted out before Luke could answer.

"He's in the trap? Well, why didn't you say so?" Cinderella exclaimed. She rushed out of the room with the mice at her heels and headed straight for the rusty old mousetrap at the bottom of the stairs. Inside the trap, a plump brown mouse cowered in a corner.

"The poor little thing is scared to death," Cinderella said.

She opened the door, and Jaq entered cautiously. "Take it easy," Jaq reassured the newcomer, who was trying to back even farther away. "There's nothing to worry about. Cinderella is our friend. She likes you. We all like you."

6

Cinderella flashed the frightened mouse a bright smile, and he finally smiled back and relaxed a little. "That's better," Cinderella said as Jaq led the new mouse out of the trap. "We have to give you a name. How about Octavius? Gus for short!"

By the smile on the new mouse's face, Cinderella knew she had made a good choice—and a new friend.

"Now I've got to get to work. See that Gus keeps out of trouble, Jaq," Cinderella said as she turned to leave. "And don't forget to warn him about the cat!"

"Have you ever seen a cat?" Jaq asked after Cinderella had gone.

Gus looked confused. "A cat?" he repeated.

"Lucifer, that's him," Jaq explained. "He's mean and sneaky." Jaq curled his fingers to imitate a cat's claws. "He'll jump at you and bite you! He's big—big as a house!"

"Lucifer," Gus said thoughtfully. He planned on staying far, far away from him.

Chapter Two

The second-floor hallway was dark and desolate until Cinderella walked to the window and opened the heavy drapes, letting in a flood of morning sunlight. She stepped up to the first of three closed doors, hesitated for a moment, took a deep breath, and opened it. In the darkness of her stepmother's bedroom Cinderella could hardly see the elaborate round cat bed where a fat black cat was sleeping.

"Here, kitty, kitty," Cinderella called softly from the doorway.

The cat slowly climbed to his feet, yawned, stretched, and gave Cinderella a disdainful look before turning his back and lying down again.

"Lucifer, come here!" Cinderella hissed impatiently.

Only then did the cat slowly and reluctantly get up from his bed and saunter across the floor.

"I'm sorry if Your Highness objects to an early breakfast," Cinderella said sarcastically. "It's certainly not my idea to feed you first. I'm just following orders. Now, come on." She started down the stairs with Lucifer close behind her.

When Cinderella entered the kitchen, the room was dark. She opened the door to let in the sunlight, then knelt beside the big brown dog stretched out on the floor. "Bruno, it's time to wake up," she urged him quietly. He awoke with a start from his dreams of chasing Lucifer.

Cinderella went back to the kitchen door and stepped out into the beautiful bright day. Every morning she looked forward to feeding her animal friends their breakfast. Now they rushed toward her from every direction as she tossed handfuls of corn into the yard. "Breakfast time!" she called. "Everybody up!"

Jaq, Luke, Gus, and the other mice gathered up bits of corn to carry back to their homes. Gus was so intent on carrying his breakfast that he didn't notice a huge dark shadow looming over him as he reentered the house. The other mice scattered in fear while Gus continued across the floor, balancing a precarious pile of corn in his arms.

When Lucifer sprang into action, Gus saw him coming just in the nick of time. The plump little mouse dropped his corn and scampered up onto the kitchen table. He leaned against a teacup to catch his breath, thinking he was safe.

But Lucifer was reaching up stealthily behind him. The cat suddenly grabbed the cup and slammed it down over the startled mouse. Lucifer's mouth stretched into an evil grin. Now Gus was right where Lucifer wanted him.

Claws at the ready, the cat carefully began to lift the cup to uncover his victim. But suddenly Lucifer let the cup drop again, startled by the shrill ringing of a row of bells high on the kitchen wall. "Cinderella!" an even shriller voice called out.

"All right, all right. I'm coming," Cinderella called, rushing back into the kitchen from the barnyard.

"Cinderella!" another voice shrieked, followed by more of the piercing bells.

"Cinderella!" a third voice shouted.

"Coming!" Cinderella cried. It was the same thing every morning. Her stepmother and stepsisters wanted their breakfast. Cinderella hurried over to the table and grabbed the three tea trays she had prepared, including the one on which Gus was trapped. Lucifer followed her out of the kitchen, eyeing the teacup Gus was under.

Cinderella climbed to the second floor and entered the first doorway in the hall. "Good morning, Drizella," Cinderella greeted her stepsister cheerfully. Cinderella always made an effort to be nice—even though her stepsisters rarely made the same effort in return. "Sleep well?"

Her thin, homely stepsister sat up in bed. Drizella's dark hair stood on end, and her pointed features were pinched into a frown. "Hmmph!" Drizella grumbled. "As if you cared." She snatched one of the trays from Cinderella's hands, then dumped a basket of wrinkled clothing at her feet. "Take that ironing and have it back in an hour," she commanded. "One hour, do you hear me?"

"Yes, Drizella," Cinderella replied. Balancing the basket on one hip,

she left the room and moved down the hall to the next bedroom.

"Good morning, Anastasia," Cinderella said as she entered.

"Well, it's about time," Anastasia muttered. Like Drizella, Anastasia was thin and homely. Her wiry red hair was a mess, and her sickly pale skin was whiter than her bed linens. She shoved another basket into Cinderella's arms. "Don't forget the mending. And don't be all day getting it done, either!"

"Yes, Anastasia," Cinderella said.

She hurried down the hall to the third room. She opened the door and greeted her stepmother. Beyond the light of the doorway, the room was dark and forbidding.

Lady Tremaine's cold voice cut through the blackness. "Don't just

stand there, child. Put that down. Then pick up the laundry and get on with your duties."

"Yes, Stepmother," Cinderella answered. She left the room and shut the door behind her. Carrying the heavy piles of ironing, mending, and laundry, she walked back down the hall. She was almost at the stairs when a terrible scream rang out from the second room.

Lucifer turned and raced down the hall to Anastasia's closed door, smiling in anticipation. As Anastasia continued to shriek, Gus ran out from under the door—right into Lucifer's waiting paws.

Cinderella rushed to Anastasia's room to see what the trouble was. "*You* did it!" Anastasia screeched, throwing open the door and pointing an accusing finger at Cinderella. "You did it on purpose!"

Chapter Three

Mother!" Anastasia howled. She ran into Lady Tremaine's room and closed the door.

Drizella emerged from her room and gave Cinderella a withering glance. "*Now* what did you do?" she snapped. Then she hurried after her sister into her mother's room.

"She put it there!" Cinderella could hear Anastasia shouting, even through the closed door. "A big, fat, ugly mouse! Under my teacup!"

Cinderella turned to stare suspiciously at Lucifer, who was curled up nearby with an innocent look on his face. "All right, Lucifer. What did you do with Gus?" Cinderella asked.

Lucifer opened his empty paws and smiled slyly.

"Oh, you're not fooling anybody," Cinderella said, picking up the big cat and shaking him out like a dusty mop. And there, under his hind foot, quivering and shivering, was Gus.

"Poor Gus," Cinderella said as the little creature scooted between her feet and disappeared into a hole in the wall. She sighed and turned back to the cat. "Oh, Lucifer. Won't you ever learn? Sometimes I wonder what I—"

"Cinderella!" Lady Tremaine's cross voice interrupted.

"Coming," Cinderella answered. She walked toward her step-mother's bedroom. Both her stepsisters had come out and were hovering in the hallway. Lucifer slipped into the room through the open door.

"Hmmph!" Drizella grumbled.

"Are you going to get it!" Anastasia added nastily as Cinderella entered the dim, eerie room.

"Close the door, Cinderella," Lady Tremaine said evenly from her

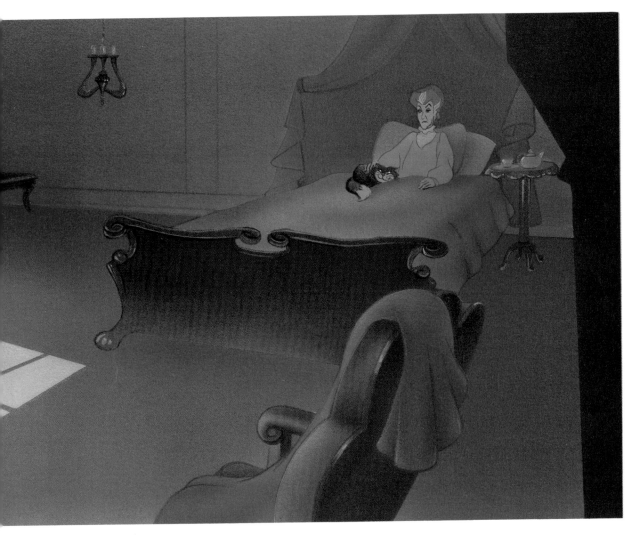

bed. She was stroking Lucifer, who had settled on her lap. Her expression was cold and malevolent.

"Oh, please," Cinderella began. "Surely you don't think that I—"

"Hold your tongue," her stepmother ordered sharply. Cinderella could see Lucifer's golden-green eyes glittering in the dimness.

Lady Tremaine picked up her teacup. "It seems we have time on our hands, Cinderella. Time for vicious practical jokes," she said. "Perhaps we can put that time to better use."

Cinderella could barely see her stepmother's cruel smile in the

shadowy darkness. She didn't know what was coming, but she was sure she wouldn't like it.

"Now, let me see," Lady Tremaine said. "There's the large carpet in the main hall—clean it! And the windows, upstairs and down—wash them! Oh, yes, the tapestries and draperies, too."

"But I just finished—," Cinderella began.

"Do them again!" her stepmother interrupted, glaring at her. "And don't forget to weed the garden, scrub the terrace, sweep the halls and the stairs, and clean the chimneys. And of course there's still the

mending, ironing, and laundry to be done." She paused for a breath and took a sip of tea. "Oh, yes, one more thing . . ."

Lucifer looked up at his mistress, eager to hear what other chores she had in mind for Cinderella. "See that Lucifer gets his bath," Lady Tremaine finished. Lucifer frowned in annoyance.

Cinderella walked out of her stepmother's room, her shoulders slumped in dejection. She had never felt so frustrated and angry. Despite all her wishes, hopes, and dreams, it seemed as if her life just kept getting worse.

Chapter Four

Meanwhile, inside the sparkling white castle that Cinderella could see through her bedroom window—if she had the time to look!—the portly, white-haired king was slumped on his throne.

"It's high time my son got married and settled down," he proclaimed to his closest adviser, the grand duke.

"Of course, Your Majesty," the grand duke answered. "But we must be patient."

"I am patient!" the king shouted impatiently. "But I'm not getting any younger, you know. I want to see my grandchildren before I go." The king calmed down, then continued sadly, "You don't know what it means to see your only child grow older and farther away from you. You don't know how lonely I am in this desolate old place." He wiped a tear from his eye. "I want to hear the pitter-patter of little feet again."

"Now, now," said the grand duke sympathetically. "Perhaps if we just let him alone . . ."

"Let him alone!" the king bellowed. "Him and his silly romantic ideas?"

"But sire," the grand duke protested timidly. "In matters of love—"

"Love!" The king cut him off. "Hah! What is love? Just a boy meeting a girl under the right conditions. So, we must simply arrange the conditions."

"But—but Your Majesty," the grand duke stammered. "How? And if the prince should even suspect, I'm sure he wouldn't—"

"Bah!" the king said in disgust. "The boy is coming home today, isn't he? Well, what could be more natural than a ball to celebrate his return?" He smiled. "And if all the eligible maidens in my kingdom just

happened to be there, he'd be bound to show interest in one of them. Wouldn't he?"

"Yes, sire," the grand duke agreed halfheartedly. In truth, he wasn't convinced at all that the king's plan would work, but he didn't want him to start shouting again. He hated it when the king got angry.

The king giggled happily, imagining the scene. "We'll have soft lights, romantic music, all the trimmings! It can't possibly fail."

"Very well, sire. I shall arrange the ball," the grand duke said.

"Make it tonight!" the king commanded. "And see that *every* eligible maiden is there!"

Chapter Five

Cinderella hummed softly to herself as she scrubbed the floor in the foyer of the château. As she worked, she dreamed of happier days long ago with her father, and she fantasized about someday being as free as the soap bubbles that wafted into the air as she scrubbed. Her reverie was interrupted by a loud knocking at the door.

"Open in the name of the king," a voice boomed. Cinderella opened the door, and a messenger handed her a large white envelope. "An urgent message from His Majesty." The messenger spun on his heel and left.

As Cinderella turned from the door, gazing curiously at the letter, Jaq and Gus poked their heads out of a mousehole. "What's it say?" they squeaked in unison.

"I don't know," Cinderella replied, examining the king's seal. "But he said it's urgent. I'd better take it up right away."

Cinderella walked up the stairs to the music room, where her stepsisters were having their lessons. She stepped cautiously into the room.

"Cinderella! I've warned you never to interrupt us," her stepmother scolded her harshly.

"But this just arrived—from the palace," Cinderella explained, holding out the white envelope.

"From the palace!" Anastasia gasped. Both sisters rushed over to Cinderella.

"Give it here!" Drizella demanded, grabbing the letter.

"No, let me have it!" Anastasia plucked it out of her sister's hands.

"No! It's mine!" Drizella shrieked. "You give that back!"

"*I'll* take it," their mother said, putting an end to the argument. She tore open the letter and read it. "Well," she said, "it seems there's to be a ball."

"A ball!" Anastasia and Drizella shrieked in unison.

Their mother nodded. "In honor of His Highness, the prince. And by royal command, every eligible maiden is to attend."

"Why, that's us," Drizella said eagerly.

"And I'm *so* eligible," Anastasia added with a sigh.

For a moment Cinderella said nothing. She was too stunned to

speak. It seemed that this day would turn out to be special after all. " 'Every eligible maiden' . . . why, that means that I can go, too," she said at last.

"Ha!" Drizella laughed, and poked her sister in the side. "Could you imagine *her* dancing with the prince? Ha!"

"I'd be honored, Your Highness," Anastasia said mockingly. "Would you mind holding my broom?" The sisters collapsed into a fit of giggles at the thought.

"Well, why not?" Cinderella said defensively. She couldn't believe that even her stepsisters were mean enough to want to rob her of a single night of happiness. "After all, I am a member of the family. And it does say 'by royal command, every eligible maiden is to attend.' "

"Yes, so it does," Lady Tremaine said slowly. "Well, I see no reason why you can't go—"

"Mother!" Drizella and Anastasia cried out in shock.

"—if," their mother went on, with a crafty look in her eye, "*if* you get all of your work done . . ."

"Oh, I will," Cinderella promised happily. The news of the ball was the most wonderful thing to happen in Cinderella's life since before her father had died. Nothing was going to make her miss this night.

". . . *and* if you can find something suitable to wear," her stepmother finished.

"I'm sure I can come up with something!" Cinderella said joyfully as she hurried out of the room. "Thank you!"

"Mother! Do you realize what you just said?" Drizella complained after Cinderella had left the room.

"Of course," her mother replied coolly. "I said 'if'!"

"Oh, *if*," Drizella said slyly as she and her sister realized what their mother had in mind.

Chapter Six

A few minutes later Cinderella rummaged through the trunk at the foot of her bed and pulled out a cloud of bright pink silk. As she held it up against her shoulders, the fabric unfurled into a long, full gown. Still holding the dress in front of her, she whirled around the room, imagining what it would be like to dance the night away at the ball. Perhaps she would sip some champagne while strolling through the palace garden under the stars. Perhaps she would meet the gentle, loving young man of her dreams. Cinderella could hardly contain her excitement.

"Isn't it lovely?" Cinderella said aloud as she held up the dress once more. "It was my mother's," she said wistfully to the crowd of mice and birds who had gathered to see what she was doing.

The animals looked on in awe. "Beautiful," one of the mice said. "But it looks kind of old."

"Well, maybe it is a bit old-fashioned," Cinderella admitted. "But I can fix that." She took a pattern book out of her sewing basket.

"There ought to be lots of good ideas in here," she said as she thumbed through the pages. "Like this one!"

She held out the book for her friends to see. There, on the opened page, was a picture of a stylish ball gown.

"Oh, that's a nice one," one of the mice said.

"Of course, I'll have to shorten the sleeves," Cinderella said thoughtfully. "And I'll need a sash, and a ruffle, and something for the collar, and—"

"Cinderella!" a voice suddenly shrieked from below.

Cinderella sighed and put down the pattern book. "Oh, now what do they want?" she asked woefully.

"Cinderella! Cinderella!" the angry voice persisted.

"All right, all right. I'm coming," Cinderella answered impatiently. "I guess my dress will have to wait," she said sadly, stroking the pink silk one last time.

"Poor Cinderella!" Jaq said as Cinderella left the room. "She won't be able to go to the ball. That's their plan. They'll make her work, work, work. Cinderella will never get her dress done in time!"

"Poor Cinderella," Gus agreed sadly.

All the birds and mice were silent for a moment, wondering what to do. A mouse named Blossom scampered over to study the pattern book Cinderella had left behind.

Suddenly Blossom smiled. "We can do it!" she piped up. "We can help Cinderella fix her dress! There's nothing to it, really. We can do it! Our Cinderella will look so beautiful!"

All the other animals jumped up and surrounded the small mouse as she began assigning them jobs. "Hurry, hurry! You can do the measuring, and we can do the sewing." She turned to Jaq and Gus. "And you two can go out and gather the trimmings."

Jaq nodded and turned to Gus. "Follow me," he said. "I know where to go!" The two mice sped off to accomplish their mission. Their first stop was Anastasia's room.

As the two mice peeked into the room from a hole in the wall, they saw Anastasia, Drizella, and Lady Tremaine giving Cinderella more chores.

Anastasia was tossing clothes on top of a heap Cinderella was balancing in her arms. "And these, too, Cinderella, and don't forget to—"

"Cinderella, take my dress," Drizella interrupted, adding another garment to the pile.

"Mend the buttonholes! Press my skirt! Mind the ruffles—you're always tearing them!" As Anastasia and Drizella kept shrieking orders to their stepsister, Jaq and Gus couldn't tell which sister was saying what anymore.

Then Cinderella's stepmother came forward. "And Cinderella," she said with a sneer. "When you're through with all that—and before

you begin your regular chores—I have a few more little things for you to do."

With her face barely visible above the towering pile of clothes, Cinderella could manage only a weak "Very well." She walked out of the room with her shoulders slumped. Jaq and Gus could see that there were tears shining in her blue eyes. Cinderella truly looked as though her heart was breaking.

Jaq and Gus remained where they were as Anastasia started to complain loudly. "Mother, I don't see why everybody else has such nice things to wear and I always end up in these old rags. Just look at this!" She held up a lovely pink sash. "Why, I wouldn't be seen dead in it," she cried, throwing it down on the floor and stalking out of the room.

"She should talk," Drizella whined. "Look at these beads!" She tossed a sparkling necklace on top of the sash. "Trash! I'm sick of them." She, too, marched out of the room, with her mother right behind her.

As soon as the door closed behind them, the two mice hopped out of their hiding place and ran over to the discarded sash and necklace.

"We can use these!" Jaq exclaimed in delight.

Gus nodded eagerly.

Just then the two mice noticed a black ball of fur curled on top of a footstool just inches away. At that same moment Lucifer woke up, spotted them, and pounced. Jaq and Gus grabbed the sash and scurried back to the mousehole, popping through it just in time to escape Lucifer's claws.

Jaq and Gus looked at each other. They had the sash—now what about the beads? They peered out of the hole and saw that Lucifer was perched right on top of the shiny necklace, a smug look on his face.

Jaq acted quickly. He dashed out and started to pull the buttons off one of Anastasia's dresses. Lucifer hesitated, glancing over at Gus waiting in the mousehole, but the temptation was too great for the cat to resist. While Lucifer leaped after Jaq, Gus rushed out and grabbed the beads. A moment later both mice were once again safely back in the mousehole, along with Drizella's discarded beads.

Jaq and Gus gathered up the sash and the beads and scrambled back to Cinderella's room, where they found a gang of mice and birds busily working on the dress. They were measuring, marking, and cutting while others sewed, snipped, or studied the pattern book. Jaq and Gus proudly draped the pink silk sash around the waist of the dress, and two birds tied it in a big beautiful bow. Then more birds laid the gleaming strand of beads at the collar.

Slowly but surely the beautiful dress was coming to life. It was hard work, but they all knew it would be worth it. They were making it possible for their friend Cinderella to attend the ball—and maybe make some of her dreams come true.

Chapter Seven

As evening fell, every maiden in the kingdom was bustling with excitement. Every maiden except one, that is.

Cinderella stood in the upstairs hall gazing forlornly out the window. She had finally managed to finish her chores. There had been no time for her to fix her dress, and the carriage was due to arrive at any moment to take Lady Tremaine and her daughters to the ball.

Cinderella sighed. It just didn't seem fair. She worked so hard and asked so little. . . . But there was no sense in spending any more time wishing for something that wasn't to be.

She was about to turn away from the window when she heard the clip-clop of horse's hooves approaching. As the sound grew louder, a gleaming black carriage being pulled by a proud white horse came into view and stopped in front of the château. Cinderella sighed, left the window, and headed down the hall.

"The carriage is here," she announced, knocking softly on her step-mother's door.

"Why, Cinderella," Lady Tremaine said as she opened the door. She looked her stepdaughter up and down, pretending to be surprised. "You aren't dressed for the ball."

"I'm not going," Cinderella nearly whispered. "I didn't have time to fix my dress."

"Oh, what a shame!" her stepmother said. She turned and smiled triumphantly at Drizella and Anastasia, who were primping by the mirror. They smirked back. "But of course there will be other times," Lady Tremaine added, turning back to face Cinderella.

"Yes," Cinderella said, fighting back tears. "Good night."

Cinderella hurried upstairs to her room. She couldn't bear to stay downstairs and watch her stepsisters and stepmother leave for the ball—the wonderful, magical ball that Cinderella herself was going to miss. Without turning on the light, she walked straight to the window and stared out at the palace on the horizon.

"Oh well, what's a royal ball?" she said aloud into the darkness. "After all, I suppose it would be frightfully dull . . . and bor-

ing . . . and completely . . . completely *wonderful,*" she admitted sadly.

Suddenly the room lit up behind her. As Cinderella spun around in surprise, two bluebirds circled the room. Then they pushed back a screen to reveal the most beautiful dress Cinderella had ever seen. "Oh my goodness," she said, stunned. "Why, it's my—"

"Surprise!" the mice squeaked, popping out of their hiding places.

"Surprise!" the birds chirped.

Cinderella was speechless. Could it be? Might she really be able to go to the ball after all? "Why, I never dreamed," she finally cried out. "This is such a wonderful surprise!" Holding the dress in front of her, she smiled at her friends and murmured, "How can I ever thank you?"

Moments later Cinderella was dressed in her beautiful new gown. She glanced out the window. The coach was still there—she wasn't too late. "Wait!" she cried, hurrying down the stairs. "Please! Wait for me!"

Lady Tremaine and her daughters were nearly out the door when Cinderella caught up to them. "Isn't it lovely?" Cinderella exclaimed,

twirling before them so that the skirt of her gown swirled out around her. "Do you like it? Do you think it will do?"

Anastasia and Drizella glared at Cinderella. "Mother!" both girls cried.

"She can't—," Anastasia howled.

"She wouldn't—," Drizella shrieked.

"Girls! Please!" Lady Tremaine shouted. "After all," she said more calmly, "we did make a bargain." She took a step toward Cinderella and stared straight into her eyes. "Didn't we?"

Cinderella smiled uncertainly.

"And I never go back on my word," her stepmother muttered thoughtfully, looking long and hard at Cinderella's dress. "How very clever, these beads. They give it just the right touch. Don't you think so?" she said sharply, turning to Drizella.

"No, I don't," Drizella said grumpily. "I think she's—" Suddenly Drizella's jaw dropped as she recognized the beads she'd thrown away. "Why, you little thief!" she screeched at Cinderella. "They're my beads! Give them here!" Drizella reached out and ripped the beads right off Cinderella's neck.

"And that's my sash! She's wearing my sash!" Anastasia shouted, tearing the sash from Cinderella's waist.

Cinderella stood between the sisters, dazed. "Oh, no, please, don't—"

But her two stepsisters continued to tear her dress apart.

Drizella grabbed a handful of the skirt. "You horrible sneak!" she screamed.

Anastasia yanked at a seam. "Ungrateful wretch!" she shrieked.

They pawed and pulled, they tugged and wrenched, they clawed and scratched . . . until Cinderella stood wearing only pink tatters and shreds.

Chapter Eight

Blinded by tears, Cinderella ran out of the house and across the yard, past the horse, past Bruno the dog, past Gus and Jaq and all her friends. When she finally reached the garden, she threw herself down on a bench in the shadows under a willow and buried her face in her arms. She had never felt so hopeless. She vowed then and there not to believe in dreams anymore, or in happiness or hope, either. Instead she resigned herself to living a miserable life of drudgery and pain.

"It's just no use," she sobbed. "No use at all! There's nothing left to believe in . . . nothing!"

"Nothing, my dear?" a melodious voice asked. "Oh, now, you don't really mean that."

"Oh, but I do!" Cinderella insisted. She lifted her head and caught her breath. A moment ago the garden had been dark and deserted. But now a smiling white-haired woman was seated on the bench, surrounded by a circle of sparkling light.

The woman helped Cinderella to her feet. Wiping a tear from Cinderella's face, she said, "Nonsense, child. If you had lost all of your

faith, I couldn't be here. But, as you can see, here I am! Now, dry those tears. You can't go to the ball looking like that."

"The ball?" Cinderella repeated, tears welling up in her eyes again. "I'm not going to the ball."

"Of course you are," the woman assured her cheerfully. "But we'll have to hurry. Even miracles take a little time, you know."

Cinderella shook her head in confusion. "Miracles?" she asked.

"Just watch," the woman said brightly. She paused, and a puzzled look crossed her face. "Now, what in the world did I do with my magic wand?"

"Magic wand," Cinderella repeated in amazement. "Why, then you must be—"

"Your fairy godmother, of course!" the woman finished for her. Then, with a wave of her hand, she magically produced a wand from

thin air. "Now, let's see," she went on. "I'd say the first thing you need is . . ."—her eyes scanned the garden—". . . a pumpkin!"

"A pumpkin?" Cinderella repeated doubtfully. She had been expecting the woman to say something about her ruined gown.

"Now for the magic words," the fairy godmother said. "Um, uh . . ." She turned toward a big round pumpkin at the edge of the garden and waved her wand. "Oh, yes, I remember: Salaga-doola, menchicka-boola, bibbidi-bobbidi-boo!"

Cinderella could hardly believe what happened next. As the fairy godmother waved her wand and sang out the magic words, the pumpkin shivered . . . and jumped . . . and expanded—and suddenly, with a jolt, the ordinary pumpkin was transformed into a magnificent, gleaming, extraordinary coach.

Cinderella gasped, and she heard smaller gasps all around her. She

saw that all her animal friends had gathered from the house and barn-yard. They looked as amazed as she was at what they had just seen.

But the fairy godmother wasn't finished yet. "Now," she continued. "To draw an elegant coach like that, of course, we'll simply have to have"—and letting her gaze roam over and then past the family's eager-looking horse, she concluded—"mice!"

With another wave of her wand and some more magic words she turned Gus, Jaq, and two other mice into sleek horses.

"Now, where were we? Oh goodness, yes. You can't go to the ball without a coachman." With that, she turned the horse into a well-dressed coachman. Then she turned to Bruno. "As for you, you'll be a footman tonight," she said. And the big brown dog was changed into just that.

The fairy godmother turned to Cinderella. "Well, well, hop in, my dear. We mustn't waste time."

Cinderella hesitated and looked down at her torn dress. "But, uh . . ."

"Now, don't try to thank me," the fairy godmother said.

"Oh, I wasn't," Cinderella began, still astonished at the magic she had just witnessed. "I mean, I do," she added quickly. "But don't you think my dress . . ."

The fairy godmother finally took a good look at Cinderella's tat-tered gown and let out a shriek of dismay. "Good heavens, child," she exclaimed. "You can't go in that!"

Cinderella smiled and shook her head.

One last time the fairy godmother fluttered her magic wand and sang out the magic words. Suddenly Cinderella felt the force of the fairy godmother's magic surrounding her. She looked down and saw that the tattered remains of her pink dress had been transformed into a stunning, shimmering, silvery gown that gleamed in the moonlight.

With matching long gloves, a black velvet choker, and a sparkling
diamond tiara, Cinderella looked like a princess. On her feet were a
pair of dainty glass slippers. She rushed over to admire her reflection
in a nearby fountain. Cinderella had never felt so beautiful.

She felt her heart fill up once again with hope and faith and delight.
"Why, it's like a dream—a wonderful dream come true!"

"Yes, my child," the fairy godmother said tenderly. "But like all
dreams, I'm afraid this one can't last forever. You'll have only until
midnight, and then—"

"Midnight!" Cinderella cried gratefully. "Oh, thank you!"

"You must understand, my dear," the fairy godmother continued seriously. "On the twelfth stroke of midnight, the spell will be broken, and everything will be as it was before."

"I understand," Cinderella said happily. "But it's so much more than I ever hoped for."

"Bless you, my child." The fairy godmother smiled and waved Cinderella into the coach.

Chapter Nine

The grand ballroom of the palace was crowded with dozens of excited young maidens from all over the kingdom. As each young lady entered the hall, the royal chamberlain announced her and introduced her to the handsome young prince, who stood on a dais at one end of the room.

As maiden after maiden came in and curtsied, the prince found himself stifling yawn after yawn. He couldn't understand why his father was making such a fuss over him by hosting this ball—or why the king was so eager to introduce him to all these young ladies. The prince didn't have any trouble meeting young ladies on his own; he just had trouble meeting anyone he felt he could care about.

He raised a hand to cover yet another yawn. The chamberlain cleared his throat as the next two young ladies approached the dais. "The mademoiselles Drizella and Anastasia Tremaine, daughters of Lady Tremaine," he announced.

The prince bowed politely to the two homely girls, who were practically tripping over their own feet as they curtsied. As he straightened up again, his gaze wandered past them to another young lady

who had just entered at the far end of the hall and was looking around uncertainly.

He stared, transfixed. She was the most beautiful girl he had ever seen. She was wearing a shimmering gown and a sparkling tiara. Her golden hair was piled atop her head, framing her lovely face. The prince suddenly had the feeling that this night might not turn out to be hopelessly boring after all. He stepped down from the dais and pushed his way between the startled Anastasia and Drizella, his eyes never leaving the maiden in the silvery gown.

Cinderella was overwhelmed by the beauty and grandeur of the palace. She felt almost dizzy as she looked around. The sound of rapidly approaching footsteps brought her back to reality. She looked up and caught her breath as she found herself gazing into the deep brown eyes of a tall, broad-shouldered young gentleman. When he gave her a kind smile and politely asked her to dance, Cinderella was astonished. She could hardly believe she was already being asked to dance—especially by someone so handsome. She had been hoping to get a look at the prince, but she decided that that could wait. She was

sure that even the prince couldn't possibly be any more handsome than this charming young man.

She returned his smile and gave him her hand. As the gentleman kissed her hand and swept her off into a waltz, Cinderella felt as though she really were living a dream—no, it was even better than a dream. It was as if she and this handsome stranger had been dancing together forever. And she knew without his saying so that he felt the same way. Without even knowing each other's name, the two young people were quickly falling in love.

As the beautiful young couple swayed wordlessly to the music, the other guests looked on—some with pleasure, and some with envy.

"Who is she, Mother?" Anastasia asked peevishly.

Drizella was trying to get a good look at the prince's partner, but such a crowd had gathered that she could catch only brief glimpses of her. "Do we know her?" she added.

"I know I've seen her before," Anastasia said.

With narrowed eyes, Lady Tremaine watched the couple dance.

"There is something familiar about her," she said slowly. She left her daughters and moved through the crowd, trying to get a closer look. But a moment later the prince led his partner out of the room and toward the royal gardens. Lady Tremaine tried to follow but found her path blocked by the grand duke, who had been ordered by the king to see that the young couple had all the privacy they needed. Frustrated, Lady Tremaine returned to the ballroom, puzzling over her strange feeling that she'd seen the beautiful young lady somewhere before.

Meanwhile, Cinderella and the prince danced across the terrace and then walked hand in hand into the moonlit garden. They strolled across a romantic little bridge, pausing in the middle to watch the sparkling water drifting by below. Cinderella looked up at the handsome young man, her eyes filled with the same love she could see reflected in his own. A moment later their lips met in a long, tender kiss.

They were interrupted by the sound of a chime from the clock tower. Cinderella broke away from the prince's embrace and glanced up at the clock, startled. "Oh my goodness!" she exclaimed. "It's midnight!" She realized she had completely lost track of the time. At the twelfth stroke of the clock all the fairy godmother's magic would be undone.

"Yes, so it is," the prince replied. "But—"

"Good-bye," Cinderella whispered, tearing herself away from his embrace.

"No! Wait! You can't go now," the prince protested.

"But I must," Cinderella replied as the clock struck again. "Please, I must!"

"But why?" the prince asked, confused by her urgency.

Cinderella desperately searched her mind for an excuse. "Well, I, uh, I haven't met the prince yet," she stammered. She turned and rushed off through the garden toward the palace.

The prince stared after her. "The prince?" he repeated with a puzzled frown. "But didn't you know—" Could she really not have known that *he* was the prince? "Wait! Come back!" he called, rushing after her. "Oh, please come back! I don't even know your name—how will I find you?"

As the clock continued to strike, Cinderella reached the palace and

rushed through the ballroom past the grand duke, who had dozed off while guarding the door to the garden. He woke with a start. "Oh, I say! Young lady, wait!"

The grand duke joined the prince in his chase, but Cinderella was already hurrying down the wide front steps of the palace toward her waiting coach. She held up her skirt so she wouldn't trip, but as she ran, one foot suddenly came out of its glass slipper. Cinderella turned to retrieve the shoe, but just then she saw the grand duke burst through the door and run toward her.

"Oh, bless me," he gasped. "Young lady, just a moment!"

Cinderella turned and ran, leaving the slipper lying where it had fallen on the steps. As the grand duke shouted for the guards to follow her, she threw herself into her carriage and sped off into the night. Down the winding hill and over a rickety bridge the carriage clattered, wildly pursued by the king's guards. Cinderella could hear the palace clock as it continued its striking: nine . . . ten . . . eleven . . .

At the stroke of midnight, the spell was instantly broken. The coach turned back into a pumpkin and the horses into mice. Bruno and the horse returned to their usual forms as well. Hearing the guards approaching, Cinderella and her animal friends jumped into the brush beside the road, shaken but unharmed.

The pumpkin was not so lucky. The thundering hooves of the guards' horses smashed it into a thousand pieces as they sped by on the road. To Cinderella's relief, the guards didn't see her.

"I'm sorry," Cinderella told her friends after the guards had passed. "I guess I forgot about everything, even the time. But it was so wonderful! And he was so handsome! And when we danced . . ."

She sighed at the memory. "I'm sure the prince himself couldn't have been more charming." She sighed again, sadly. "And I don't even know his name. I'll probably never see him again."

She looked down at her tattered old dress and saw, peeking out from under the skirt, one bare foot . . . and one sparkling glass slipper. Cinderella gasped and reached down to remove the slipper. She cradled it gently in her hands, overjoyed to have a memento of the most marvelous evening of her life.

She looked up at the starry sky, thinking of the kind fairy godmother who had made it all possible. "Thank you!" she cried out joyously. "Thank you so very much . . . for everything!"

Chapter Ten

The next morning the grand duke stood nervously outside the king's bedroom. Summoning all his courage, he knocked gingerly on the door. The king had left the ball soon after the prince and Cinderella had started dancing, so he didn't yet know about the girl's hasty exit. The grand duke wished more than anything that he didn't have to be the one to give the king the news.

"Come in!" the king called.

The grand duke slowly opened the door and peeked inside.

The king sat up in bed and wiped the sleep from his eyes. When he saw the grand duke he jumped out of bed. "So! Has he proposed already?" he asked jubilantly. "Tell me all about it. Who is she? Where does she live?"

"W-well," the grand duke stammered, "I didn't get a chance to—"

"No matter. We have more important things to discuss—arrangements for the wedding, invitations, all those sorts of things."

The grand duke gulped. "But—"

"Here, have a cigar," the king said, shoving one into the grand duke's mouth. "To celebrate the marriage of my son, and your knighthood."

"Knighthood?" the grand duke repeated, tears welling in his eyes. He couldn't stand it any longer. He had to tell the king the truth. "Sire, she got away," he blurted out.

The king's face turned crimson as the meaning of the words sank in. "She what?" he bellowed.

"I tried to stop her," the grand duke cried. "But she vanished into thin air."

"A likely story," the king said, rushing across the room and grabbing his sword.

"But it's true, sire," the grand duke insisted, his hands trembling as he pulled out the slipper he had picked up from the steps. "All we could find was this glass slipper."

"The whole thing was a plot," the king shouted, swiping vigorously at the grand duke with his sword.

The grand duke ducked. "But your son loves her," he explained quickly. "He won't rest until he finds her. He's determined to marry her."

The king's expression softened. "He what?"

"The prince swears that he'll marry none but the girl who fits this." The grand duke held out the glass slipper in his shaking hand.

The king snatched the slipper and kissed it. He paused and scratched his chin thoughtfully. "Then," he said finally, "you will try this on every maiden in the land. And as soon as you find one this shoe fits, we will have the biggest wedding this kingdom has ever seen!"

*　*　*

It didn't take long for the news to spread. Lady Tremaine rushed to wake Anastasia and Drizella the moment she heard about the slipper.

Cinderella was preparing breakfast when she heard her stepmother shouting, "Get up, quick! This instant! Anastasia! Drizella! We haven't a moment to lose!" Cinderella hurried to finish her task, curious to discover what the fuss was about. There was such a commotion that even the mice peeked out from their holes in curiosity.

Anastasia groggily sat up in bed as her mother bustled about the room, opening the drapes and grabbing clothes from the closet. "Huh? What's going on?" she asked with a yawn.

"Everyone's talking about it," her mother said. "The whole kingdom. Hurry now. He'll be here any minute."

"Who?" Drizella asked. She was standing in the doorway, scratching herself sleepily.

"The grand duke. He's hunting for that girl, the one who lost her slipper at the ball last night," Lady Tremaine explained, just as Cinderella arrived at the door with the tea trays. "They say the prince is madly in love with her—"

Crash! The breakfast trays slipped from Cinderella's hands onto the floor. She gasped and brought her hand to her mouth. "He was the prince!" she whispered to herself.

"You clumsy little fool!" her stepmother cried. "Clean that up! And then help my daughters dress."

"What for?" Drizella said.

"That's right," Anastasia agreed grumpily. "If he's in love with that girl, what good does getting dressed up do us?"

Cinderella absentmindedly started to pick up the mess, still stunned at the news that her handsome stranger was the prince.

72

"Now you two listen to me," Lady Tremaine told her daughters sharply. "There's still a chance that one of you can get him. No one—not even the prince—knows who that girl is."

Gus and Jaq were watching and listening. "We know!" Gus squeaked excitedly. "It's Cinderella!" Jaq shushed him, anxious to hear every word.

"The glass slipper is their only clue," Lady Tremaine continued. "The grand duke has been ordered to try it on every girl in the kingdom. And if one can be found whom the slipper fits, then by the king's command that girl shall be the prince's bride."

"His bride!" the two sisters shrieked.

"His bride . . . ," Cinderella echoed softly in awe.

"Cinderella! You must get my things together right away," Drizella commanded.

"Never mind her, Cinderella," Anastasia said. She ran around the room wildly gathering up clothes. "Mend these now!"

"Not until she irons my dress," Drizella said.

Soon both girls began tossing heaps of clothing into Cinderella's arms.

Cinderella stood motionless, staring off into space with a dreamy expression on her face. Such wonderful thoughts were whirling around in her head that she could hardly take them all in. She had to be dreaming, she decided.

"What's the matter with her?" Anastasia said irritably, noticing Cinderella's distracted expression.

"Wake up, stupid. We've got to get dressed," Drizella snapped.

At the sound of her stepsisters' voices, Cinderella snapped out of her reverie. With a burst of happiness she realized that she wasn't

dreaming after all—it was all true! The gentle, handsome, charming prince really wanted to marry *her*! "Dressed," Cinderella said joyfully. "Oh, yes, we must get dressed!" Without another word Cinderella dropped the clothing and left the room, humming the tune of the waltz from the previous night.

"Mother, did you see what she did?" Drizella whined.

"Are you just going to let her walk out?" Anastasia demanded.

"Quiet!" their mother said, staring after Cinderella with narrowed eyes. She recognized that tune from the ball. Could it be? she thought. She left the room and headed down the hall toward the staircase Cinderella had just climbed.

In her room Cinderella was standing at her mirror, combing her hair, still humming. Finally, finally my dreams are to come true, she thought ecstatically. After all her years of suffering she would be happy at last. Cinderella flashed a glorious smile to the mice who had gathered around her.

Just then Cinderella looked up and caught her stepmother's reflection in the mirror. Her stepmother was standing at the bedroom door, her eyes dark, her mouth twisted in a snarl.

As Cinderella spun around, startled, she heard the sound of the door slamming and the clink of a key in the lock.

Cinderella raced across the room and pulled at the door, but it wouldn't budge. Her stepmother had locked her in.

"Please," Cinderella begged. "You can't do this! You just can't!" She threw herself against the door, crying, "Let me out! You must let me out!"

Chapter Eleven

Jaq and Gus watched with the other mice as Cinderella sobbed brokenheartedly. "We've got to get that key," Jaq said with determination. "We've just got to!" The two mice slipped under the door and quietly followed Lady Tremaine downstairs.

"Mother! He's here," Drizella cried excitedly.

"Oh, do I look all right?" Anastasia asked, primping at the mirror.

Drizella elbowed her sister aside. "What about me?"

"Girls!" their mother said. "Now remember. This is your last chance. Don't fail me." She hurried to open the door.

A royal footman stood at the threshold. "Announcing His Imperial Grace, the grand duke!" The footman waved the grand duke in with a flourish.

Lady Tremaine smiled and bowed. "May I present my daughters, Drizella and Anastasia."

The grand duke peered at the ugly stepsisters and shuddered. "Charmed, I'm sure," he said. But in reality he was already quite certain

that neither of these homely creatures could be the young lady with whom the prince had waltzed the night before.

"His Grace will read a royal proclamation," the footman announced. He pulled a scroll from his pocket, unrolled it, and held it up for the grand duke to read.

The grand duke cleared his throat. " 'All subjects of His Imperial Majesty,' " he began, taking the scroll from the footman's hands, " 'are hereby notified that in regard to a certain glass slipper . . .' "

As the grand duke continued to read, the footman held up a pillow covered by a cloth. He pulled back the cloth with a flourish, revealing the dainty glass slipper.

"Why, that's my slipper!" Drizella shrieked, rushing forward.

"What?" Anastasia cried. "Well, I like that! It's *my* slipper!"

"Girls! Girls!" their mother scolded. "Remember your manners. A thousand pardons, Your Grace," she said to the grand duke.

The grand duke cleared his throat again and read on. As Lady Tremaine listened intently, Gus and Jaq cautiously climbed up the table next to her and inched their way toward the pocket of her skirt, which contained the key to Cinderella's room. Jaq teetered on the edge of the table, and with Gus holding on to his tail, he lowered himself down into the pocket.

"Now, let us proceed with the fitting," the grand duke said at last.

"Of course," Lady Tremaine agreed. "Anastasia, dear," she called, motioning the girl to a chair.

Anastasia daintily pulled back the hem of her dress, and the footman slid the slipper right onto her bare foot.

"There!" Anastasia said triumphantly. "I knew it was my slipper. It's exactly my size. I always wear the same size. . . ."

Her voice trailed off as the footman lifted Anastasia's foot and more of the dress fell back, revealing the tiny slipper dangling off one of her huge toes.

"Oh well," said Anastasia, her face turning red. "It may be a trifle snug today. You know how it is . . . dancing all night. It's always fit perfectly before!"

But no matter how she pushed, she could not force her large, knobby foot into the dainty slipper.

"Are you sure you're trying it on the right foot?" her mother asked, bending over to help. As she did so, Jaq—and the key—came tumbling out of her pocket and onto the floor with a clank.

Luckily Anastasia and her mother were so busy struggling with the shoe that they didn't even notice. Staggering under the weight of the heavy key, Jaq and Gus headed for the stairs.

"I don't think you're half trying," Anastasia said to the footman.

"Next, please!" the duke commanded, pointing to Drizella.

By the time they reached the top of the long, steep stairway leading up to Cinderella's room, Jaq and Gus were more exhausted than they had ever been in their lives. But they knew they had to free their friend from her room before the grand duke left—her future and her happiness depended on it.

Cinderella heard a sound on the landing outside her room. She peeked through the keyhole and immediately stopped crying. For there, just outside the door, were two little mice and one big brass key.

Cinderella's face lit up in a smile when she saw Jaq squirm under her door. But the smile quickly faded when she heard a loud crash from outside. Peering out through the keyhole again, she saw Lucifer smiling smugly. He had Gus—and the key—trapped under a glass bowl.

"Lucifer! Let him go!" she pleaded. "Please, let him go!"

Jaq squeezed back under the door. He rolled up his sleeves and bravely faced his foe. "Let him out!" he squeaked, baring his teeth.

Before the cat could respond, Jaq grabbed his black furry tail and bit down hard. Lucifer shot up off the ground in surprise and pain, his paws clawing at the air. But before Jaq could free Gus, Lucifer fell back down and grabbed the bowl again.

Within seconds a whole army of Cinderella's friends came to the rescue. Mice hurled forks like spears at the sneaky cat. Birds flew

overhead, dropping dishes on his head. But despite their best efforts, Gus and the key remained trapped.

"Bruno! Get Bruno!" Cinderella cried through the keyhole.

Two bluebirds flew off to find the dog. Moments later Bruno came charging up the stairs. That did it—Lucifer took one look and ran for his life.

As soon as the coast was clear, three of the strongest mice lifted the glass bowl and freed Gus. Then Jaq and Gus picked up the key once more and dragged it under the door into Cinderella's room.

Chapter Twelve

"Of all the stupid idiots," Drizella screamed as the footman struggled to fit the glass slipper onto her gigantic foot. "I'll do it myself. I'll make it fit." She grabbed the shoe out of the footman's hands.

After moaning and groaning, squeezing and squashing and bending, Drizella finally managed to cram her foot into the slipper. "There!" she exclaimed, triumphantly holding her foot out for inspection.

"It fits?" the grand duke said in surprise. But suddenly Drizella's tortured toes uncoiled. The too-tight slipper shot off her foot and flew straight up into the air.

The grand duke and the footman both lunged to catch the fragile slipper. They bumped into each other and crashed to the floor just as the glass shoe came plummeting down to earth. Spread out flat on the floor, the grand duke reached out his hand . . . and caught the slipper on the tip of one finger.

"Oh, Your Grace, I'm dreadfully sorry," Lady Tremaine said, gazing down at the grand duke in horror. "It won't happen again."

"Precisely, madam," the grand duke replied from his awkward

position on the floor. He stood up and brushed himself off. "You are the only young ladies of the household, I hope—er, I mean, I presume," he said to Anastasia and Drizella.

"There's no one else, Your Grace," Lady Tremaine assured him.

"In that case, then, good day," the grand duke said. He was eager to leave this unpleasant household.

But just as he turned to go, a gentle voice called out from the top of the stairs. "Your Grace! Please wait!"

All eyes turned to Cinderella, who was hurrying down the stairs. "May I try it on?" she asked.

"Pay no attention to her," Lady Tremaine told the grand duke. "It's only Cinderella."

"Our scullery maid," Anastasia explained.

"From the kitchen," Drizella added.

But the grand duke was not listening to the stepfamily anymore. "Come, my child," he said to Cinderella kindly, taking her by the hand and leading her to a chair.

As soon as she was seated, the footman came running with the slipper. Suddenly an evil smile crossed Cinderella's stepmother's face. When the footman was only a few steps away from Cinderella, Lady Tremaine stuck out her cane and tripped him.

The footman and the slipper went flying. The footman fell to the floor with a thud; the slipper shattered into a million bits of broken glass on the floor at Cinderella's feet.

"Oh, no, no, no!" the grand duke cried out, falling to his knees and staring at the shards in disbelief. "This is terrible! What will the king say?"

Lady Tremaine smiled smugly. This time she was sure she had put Cinderella in her place for good.

"Perhaps," Cinderella spoke up softly, "if it would help—"

"No, no," the grand duke moaned. "Nothing can help now."

"But you see," Cinderella said, "I have the other slipper." She pulled the other glass slipper out of her pocket and handed it to the grand duke while Lady Tremaine and her daughters looked on in shock.

The grand duke grabbed the precious slipper and kissed it. He smiled at Cinderella and gently slid the dainty slipper onto her foot. It fit perfectly, of course, and both Cinderella and the grand duke laughed with delight.

Cinderella held up her foot, admiring the tiny, perfect slipper sparkling in the light. She didn't even notice her stepfamily's jealous scowls. The face of her gentle, handsome prince filled her mind, and her heart brimmed over with the knowledge that she would never be unhappy again.

Epilogue

The bells of the palace clock tower chimed merrily as Cinderella and the prince ran from the church. Two chirping bluebirds held up the train of Cinderella's beautiful white wedding gown as she smiled at the townspeople who had gathered to see the happy couple. The well-wishers showered the newlyweds with rice as they ducked into their honeymoon coach. The whole kingdom seemed to be aglow with love and goodwill.

Cinderella turned to her new husband, holding his hand tightly. As the coach carried them off to begin their new life together, Cinderella thought only of good things. She thought of the happy times she had shared with her father. She thought of her faithful animal friends at the château. She thought of the kind fairy godmother who had made her new life possible. She thought of her loving prince, with whom she would live in happiness and harmony all the days of their lives.

And finally, as the prince leaned over to kiss his new bride, Cinderella thought about how she had learned never, ever to give up on her dreams.